Charlie Cook's Favorite Book

SHIVER ME TIMBERS

FAIRY TALES
FROM A FORGOTTEN ISLAND

THE BEARO ANNUAL

JOUST JOKING!

REAL BIRDS

 For Alice, Alison, and Alyx

ISBN-13: 978-0-545-11032-7
ISBN-10: 0-545-11032-7

12 11 10 9 8 7 6 5 4 3 2 1   8 9 10 11 12 13/0

Printed in the U.S.A.   40

First Scholastic printing, September 2008

The art was created using pencil, ink, watercolors, colored pencils, and crayons.

Charlie Cook's Favorite Book

Julia Donaldson
illustrated by Axel Scheffler

SCHOLASTIC INC.
New York Toronto London Auckland Sydney
Mexico City New Delhi Hong Kong Buenos Aires

Once upon a time there was a boy
called Charlie Cook
Who curled up in a cozy chair
and read his favorite book . . .

About a leaky pirate ship
that very nearly sank
And a pirate chief who got the blame
and had to walk the plank.
The chief swam to an island
and went digging with his hook.

At last he found a treasure chest,
and in it was a book . . .

About a girl called Goldilocks,
and three indignant bears
Who cried, "Who's had our porridge?
Who's been sitting on our chairs?"

They went into the bedroom,
and Baby Bear said, "Look!
She's in my bed, and what is more,
she's got my favorite book . . ."

ABOUT SIR PERCY PILKINGTON,
A BOLD AND FEARLESS KNIGHT,
WHO TOLD THE DRAGON . . .

Wait!
I'm not quite ready
for the fight.

You must hear
this one first!

AND THEN HIS ARMOR CLANKED AND SHOOK

AS HE READ ALOUD A JOKE HE'D FOUND
(INSIDE HIS FAVORITE BOOK) . . .

About Rowena Reddalot,
   a very well-read frog,

Who jumped upon a lily pad

and jumped upon a log,

Then jumped into the library
that stood beside the brook,

30

 And went "Reddit! Reddit! Reddit!"
as she jumped upon a book . . .

About an oak tree full of birds.

Each bird had built a nest,

And they had a competition

to decide which one was best.

They chose an owl to judge it,
and the winner was a rook
Whose nest was lined with pages
from his very favorite book . . .

*A*bout a girl who saw

a flying saucer in the sky.

Some small green men were in it

and they waved as they flew by.

She tugged her mother's sleeve and said,

"Look, Mum, what I've just seen!"

But Mum said, "Hush, I'm trying to read

my favorite magazine . . ."

About a wicked jewel thief
who stole the king's best crown

But then got stuck behind some sheep, which slowed his car right down.

The king got on the phone and soon the cops had caught the crook,

And flung him into prison, where he read his favorite book ...

About a greedy crocodile

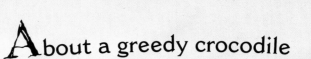

who got fed up with fish

And went on land to try to find

some other kind of dish.

He went into a bookshop
and he there grew even greedier

While reading (on page 90
of a large encyclopedia) . . .

CAKE: a mixture of nice things, usually baked in the oven. It is eaten for dessert and on special occasions like birthdays and Christmas.

THE QUEEN'S BIRTHDAY CAKE

It took six trucks to carry the Cocoa Munchies for the queen's birthday cake to the palace. The cake also required 4,276 chocolate bars and 739 bags of marshmallows. The special extra-large cake tin was made by the Royal Blacksmith, using 2,647 melted-down horseshoes.

FAMOUS CAKE-EATERS

The world's most famous cake-eaters are the Bunn twins of York, England. At the age of six they became the youngest ever winners of the York Festival Cake-Eating Competition. At ten, they had to be taken to the hospital after knocking each other out while both reaching for the same slice of cake. (Their dog then ate the cake.)

About the biggest birthday cake the world had ever seen. A team of royal cakemakers had made it for the queen.

The cake was so delicious
　　that a famous spaceman took
A slice of it to Jupiter.
　　He also took a book . . .

About a ghost who glided round a castle every night.

Carrying her head and giving everyone a fright.

She kept it up till morning, then she found a shady nook

And put her head back on again
to read her favorite book . . .

About a cozy armchair,
and a boy called Charlie Cook.

SHIVER ME TIMBERS
FAIRY TALES
FROM A FORGOTTEN ISLAND
THE BEARO ANNUAL
JOUST JOKING!
STORIES of
REAL BIRDS

A COUNTRY CHILDHOOD
TALES FOR JAILS
My First Encyclopedia
A-Z
OUT OF THIS WORLD
A COLLECTION OF GHOST STORIES